AUG 2016

PoLKa Dots
FoR PoPPy

Amy Schwartz

HOLIDAY HOUSE / NEW YORK

In memory of my mother, Eva Schwartz

Copyright © 2016 by Amy Schwartz
All Rights Reserved
HOLIDAY HOUSE is registered in the U.S. Patent and Trademark Office.
Printed and Bound in April 2016 at Toppan at Leefung, Dong Guan City, China.
The artwork was created with gouache and pen and ink.
www.holidayhouse.com
First Edition
1 3 5 7 9 10 8 6 4 2

Library of Congress Cataloging-in-Publication Data

Schwartz, Amy, author, illustrator.
Polka dots for poppy / Amy Schwartz. — First edition.
pages cm
Summary: "Three sisters help their youngest sibling get the polka-dotted
clothing that they can't find in any stores"— Provided by publisher.
ISBN 978-0-8234-3431-2 (hardcover)
[1. Clothing and dress—Fiction. 2. Sisters—Fiction.] I. Title.
PZ7.S406Po 2016
[E]—dc23
2014044021

At bedtime Mama said,
"Tomorrow we're going back-to-school shopping."

Ava said,
"I want a princess dress."

Isabelle said,
"I want a purple dress."

Charlie Ann said,
"I want a cowboy vest."

Poppy said,
"Polka Dots!"

"My princess dress," Ava said, "will be all pink and princessy. With a long princess cape and a gold pointy crown."

"My purple dress," Isabelle said, "will have twelve purple buttons and two purple pockets, and purple puffed sleeves."

"My cowboy vest," said Charlie Ann,
"will have four cowboy pockets
for four shiny apples for
Trigger, my horse."

"Polka Dots!"
said Poppy.

"Good night,
fashion plates,"
Mama said,
and turned
out the light.

All night the girls dreamed

of princessy princesses,

of puffed purple sleeves,

of horses named Trigger

and
of Polka Dots!

The next morning, bright and early,
Mama and the girls left for the mall.
When *Cinderella Shoes* opened, they were the first ones inside.

"Pink jellies!" Ava said.
"How princessly perfect!"

"Purple sneakers!"
Isabelle said.
"Do you have purple socks?"

"Cowboy boots!"
Charlie Ann said,
"with cowboy curlicues!"

But for Poppy
there were no Polka Dots.

Then up the up escalator
and into *Girly Gear*.

Ava found a princess dress
with a pink princess sash.

Then *Flirty Skirty*.
Isabelle found a purple dress
with twelve purple buttons.

And at Yippee-Ki-Ay Charlie Ann found
a cowboy vest with long cowboy fringes.

But for Poppy
there were no
Polka Dots.

Poppy sat down on her bottom.

"Poppy," Ava said, "you'd look so pretty in pink."

"Or purple," Isabelle said.

"Or in a vest," Charlie Ann said, "with fringes and pockets."

"Stripes," Mama said, "can be very nice."

"Polka Dots!" said Poppy.

"I think," Mama said, "it's time to go home."

In the van
Isabelle sang,
"Purple's spectacular!"
Ava chanted,
"Princesses rule school!"
Charlie Ann whinnied like Trigger.
Poppy said nothing at all.

After supper and stories
the girls climbed into bed.
Ava doodled dots on her
Doodle Pad.

Isabelle popped and
unpopped her pop beads.

Charlie Ann spilled a
whole box of Red Hots
on her comforter.

Poppy snored
a small baby snore.

Ava sat up.
"I've got it!"
she said.

"Me too!"
Isabelle said.

Charlie Ann said,
"Let's get to work."

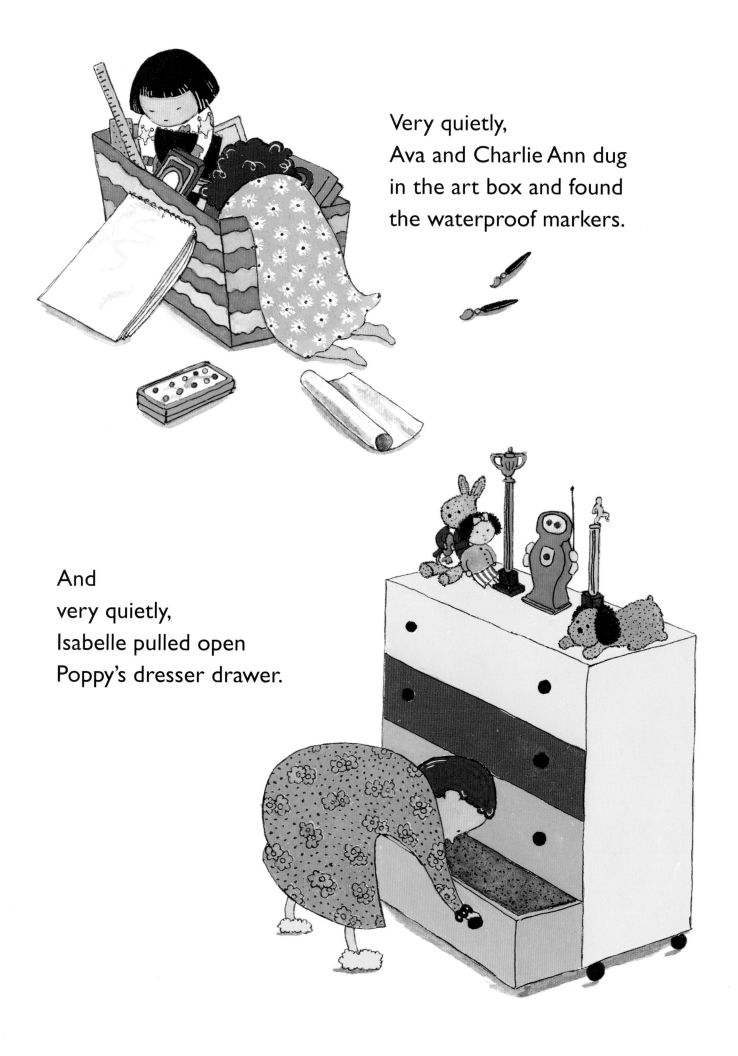

Very quietly,
Ava and Charlie Ann dug
in the art box and found
the waterproof markers.

And
very quietly,
Isabelle pulled open
Poppy's dresser drawer.

In the morning Mama woke Poppy.

"Sleepyhead, let's get you dressed."

Mama pulled open Poppy's dresser drawer.
"Sweetie," she said, "are *these* your white
shorts?"

Poppy clapped her hands.
Her white short shorts were no longer white.

Poppy's white shorts were covered
with blue
and purple
and yellow
Polka Dots!

"Oh my," Mama said.
"Oh. My."

"And, Poppy, your white strappy sandals ..."

Poppy laughed.
Her white strappy sandals were no longer white.

Her sandals were covered
with red
and red-orange
and blue-green
and green-blue
Polka Dots!

"Gracious," Mama said.
"Good gracious me."

And your white cotton play dress ..."
Poppy jumped up and down.
Her white cotton play dress was no longer white.

The play dress was covered
with pink
and magenta
and violet
and sea green
and yellow-green
and yellow-orange
and orange-yellow
and sky-blue
and midnight-blue
Polka Dots!

"Poppy," Mama said.
"Let's find your sisters."

Ava and Isabelle were
eating toast in the kitchen.
Charlie Ann was making
chocolate milk.

"Wow," Mama said.

Poppy twirled in a circle.
She twirled around twice.

Ava said, "How pretty!
Polka Dot shorts!"

Isabelle said,
"And Polka Dot sandals!"

Charlie Ann said,
"And a Polka Dot dress!
Who would have guessed?"

"Yes," Mama said.
"Who would have guessed?"

And then, after breakfast, the girls all played school.

Ava wore her princess dress and her gold pointy crown.

She looked very princessy.

Isabelle wore her purple dress with twelve purple buttons.

Charlie Ann wore her cowboy vest and her chaps.

And Poppy wore . . .

Polka Dots!